ISBN: 0-7172-8822-6

Manufactured in the United States of America.
A B C D   1 2 3 4

Disney's

Jungle Cubs

Bee a Friend

GROLIER
BOOK CLUB EDITION

Mowgli has always loved the jungle. When he was a baby, Mowgli had been lost there. The good jungle animals found and cared for him until he was old enough to go home. But even after he had returned to the man-village, Mowgli would go back to visit his animal friends in the jungle.

But there was one jungle animal who was not
Mowgli's friend. It was Shere Khan, the fierce
tiger! Shere Khan lived alone. He wanted no
friends. All he wanted was food!

"Ah, I see my dinner!" said Shere Khan,
watching Mowgli.

He sneaked up
behind Mowgli and
growled, "How nice
of you to visit me at
dinner time, boy!"
Mowgli spun
around and stared
up into the tiger's
hungry, yellow eyes.

Luckily, Mowgli's friends, Baloo, the bear, and
Bagheera, the panther, happened to be there.
   "Hey, Shere Khan, cool it!" shouted Baloo.
"Leave my buddy alone!"

"And why should I?" asked Shere Khan coldly.

"Because we saved your life!" replied Baloo with a smile.

"Nonsense," said Shere Khan. "I rule this jungle. I need no one's help!"

"You did once," Baloo continued.
"When we were cubs, remember? We
all used to play together—although you
were never much fun! One day we saved
your stripes from a wolf pack!"

"I don't remember that!"
said Shere Khan.

"Of course you do!" Bagheera
said. "It all started at the old
temple ruins. Kaa tried to hypnotize
Baloo, even though Baloo was
already asleep!"

"Yeah," agreed Baloo. "While I was sleeping, Louie was playing on a vine. Suddenly, a honey bee flew right under his nose!"

As Baloo and Bagheera told the story, Shere Khan began to remember.

The bee caused Louie to fall off the vine. When it flew past Baloo, the sleeping bear cub stood up to follow the bee. Baloo was walking in his sleep! The sound of the bee's buzzing made him dream of honey!

As he walked,
the little bear
dreamed of valleys,
rivers, and hills—
all made of sweet,
delicious honey!

Kaa and Prince Louie watched Baloo. Louie, ever the playful monkey, decided to trick Kaa. So he said to the snake, "This is all your fault! You've hypnotized Baloo. So you have to take care of him and make sure he doesn't get hurt!"

Kaa gulped and said, "Heavens! I never meant to cause trouble. I'll un-hypnotize him!"

But before Kaa could wake Baloo, the young snake saw that Baloo was heading for a cliff! So Kaa quickly made a bridge for the sleeping bear to cross!

"Ergggh!" Kaa groaned. "Hurry up! You're heavy!"

Kaa had a hard time keeping up with Baloo.
The faster the bee flew, the faster Baloo
followed it! Soon Baloo and Kaa arrived
at the bees' honey cave near the river.

Kaa caught up with Baloo.

"Baloo, listen," he said nervously. "When I snap my fingers, you will wake up. Oh, dear! I forgot. I don't have any fingers!"

Just then the bee, tired of being followed, turned around and flew straight at Baloo!

The bee stung Baloo!
"Ouch!" he cried.
Suddenly Baloo woke up.
"What happened?" he asked
in a daze. "Where am I?"

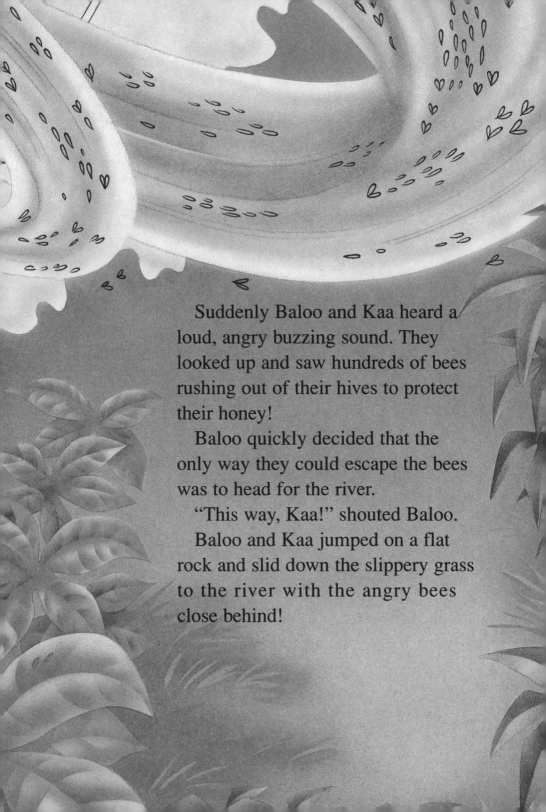

Suddenly Baloo and Kaa heard a
loud, angry buzzing sound. They
looked up and saw hundreds of bees
rushing out of their hives to protect
their honey!

Baloo quickly decided that the
only way they could escape the bees
was to head for the river.

"This way, Kaa!" shouted Baloo.

Baloo and Kaa jumped on a flat
rock and slid down the slippery grass
to the river with the angry bees
close behind!

Meanwhile, in another part of the forest, a
deer was grazing. Suddenly it lifted its nose
and sniffed the air. It caught a familiar
scent—a frightening scent! Wolves!

As the wolves chased the deer, a bird was
watching.

The bird quickly flew to its friends and warned them of the danger.

"I'm not afraid of any wolves," said Shere Khan proudly. "We tigers rule the jungle!"

Louie laughed.

"Be careful, Shere Khan," he said. "You may rule, but there's only one of you and lots of them!"

Suddenly Louie remembered that poor Baloo
was out sleepwalking somewhere with Kaa.
Louie jumped on Hathi the elephant's back.
"Hurry!" Louie cried. "We've got to find
Baloo and Kaa. We've got to warn them!"

Bagheera, Louie, and Hathi searched and searched, but Baloo and Kaa were nowhere to be found. Just as the three were about to give up hope, they saw Baloo and Kaa floating in the river!

Baloo shouted a big hello.

"You look all tense and nervous," he said to his friends. "Jump in and cool off. The water's great!"

Meanwhile, back at the temple ruins, Shere
Khan heard howling behind him. He quickly
spun around just as two wolves rushed at him!

Shere Khan was small, but he was still a tiger!
The young cub had no trouble defending himself.

But an instant later,
two more wolves
appeared! And these
were bigger and even
more vicious! Shere Khan
was in big trouble!

Shere Khan turned and jumped onto the temple wall. He was safe for the moment, but the tiger knew he would have to come down eventually. When he did, all those sharp teeth would be waiting for him! Just then, Baloo and the others appeared.

"Hey, have you flea-bitten mutts come to visit us?" Baloo asked the wolves with a laugh.

"Go home!" said Hathi, snorting loudly through his trunk.

"You don't want a tiger," laughed Louie. "Tigers don't taste good. Try this instead!"

With that, Louie threw a rotten mango right into the face of the lead wolf!

The wolves were furious! They chased
after the jungle cubs.

"Run to the honey cave!" Baloo shouted.
"I have a plan!"

"Baloo, are you sure you know what you're
doing?" Louie asked the bear.

Baloo was clever. He knew the dogs'
barking would attract the bees. The angry
insects flew out of their hives and attacked
the wolves!

The jungle cubs were smart. They jumped into the river and hid under the water until the bees passed. Then they stuck their heads up and laughed as the bees chased the wolves all the way down the river!

"It'll be a long time before we see those mangy mutts again!" laughed Baloo.

Later, when they got back to the old temple,
Baloo said to Shere Khan, "Don't bother to
thank us."

"Thank you for what?" the young tiger asked.

"For saving your skin!" answered Louie.

"And you never did thank us," Baloo said
finishing the story. "So you can do it now by
letting Mowgli go."

"It never happened!" Shere Khan growled.
"Besides, it was a long time ago and right
now I'm still hungry!"

Then the huge tiger looked at
Mowgli and slowly walked up
to the frightened boy.

Baloo knew it would take
more than words to stop
the tiger now! Baloo looked
up and saw a beehive in
the tree right above
Shere Khan.

Baloo threw a rock at the beehive.
"Heads up, Shere Khan!" Baloo shouted.
The startled Shere Khan let out a horrified gasp as
the beehive fell right on his head!

Mowgli and his friends laughed as the tiger ran
away pursued by an angry swarm of bees.

"That will teach Shere Khan some manners," said
Mowgli. "You should always thank your friends for
saving your life. Thanks everyone!"